Also by Anne Fine

Bill's New Frock

How to Write Really Badly

Saving Miss Mirabelle

Ivan the Terrible

The Angel of Nitshill Road

'The Chicken Gave it to Me'

On Planet Fruitcake

For younger readers

Press Play

Magic Ball

Friday Surprise

Under the Bed

Big Red Balloon

ANNELI THE ART HATER

ANNELI THE ART HATER

ANNE FINE

Illustrated by Vanessa Julian-Ottie

EGMONT

You can visit Anne Fine's website
www.annefine.co.uk

and download free bookplates from
www.myhomelibrary.org

EGMONT
We bring stories to life

First published in Great Britain 1986
by Methuen Children's Books
This edition published 2018
by Egmont UK Limited
The Yellow Building, 1 Nicholas Road, London W11 4AN

Text copyright © Anne Fine 1986
Illustrations copyright © Vanessa Julian-Ottie 1986

The moral rights of the author and illustrator have been asserted

ISBN 978 1 4052 8903 0

25195/1

A CIP catalogue record for this title is available from the British Library

Typeset by Avon DataSet Ltd, Bidford on Avon, Warwickshire
Printed and bound in Great Britain by the CPI Group

Stay safe online. Any website addresses listed in this book are correct at
the time of going to print. However, Egmont is not responsible for content
hosted by third parties. Please be aware that online content can be subject
to change and websites can containcontent that is unsuitable for children.
We advise that all children are supervised when using the internet

Egmont takes its responsibility to the planet and its
inhabitants very seriously. All the papers we use are from
well-managed forests run by responsible suppliers.

1

'More pink, dear?'

'More pink, dear, don't you think?'

Anneli didn't, but was too polite to say so.

Miss Pears dabbed once or twice at Anneli's painting.

'There! Much, much better. But you'll need more.'

Anneli scowled as Miss Pears turned her back and started mixing more pink. Anneli hated painting. She hated anything to do with art. She loathed messing with clay and smudging with pastels. She disliked greasy crayons and tatty scraps of material and dried pasta shells and leftover Christmas wrapping paper.

And she was bored stiff by all those endless discussions about what everyone was going to do.

'Aliens from Outer Space? What a good idea, Henry! That should get rid of some of this aluminium foil.'

She hated the chaotic sharing out of all the horrid stuff that they were going to do it with.

'Bags the glue!'

'I asked *first*!'

'No, you did *not*!'

'Swap the green lace for half those beads? Please? Pretty, pretty *please*?'

'He asked *first*!'

'No, he didn't!'

And whatever they chose in the end, Anneli hated doing it. She'd toil away, getting it finished as soon as possible, but she resented all Miss Pears' encouraging remarks as she made her way round the room, rescuing a warped drawing of a cat for one person, mixing an awkward

red-brown colour for another, breaking
up fights.

Afterwards, Anneli hated having to
show her work to her friends, especially to
Henry. She hated carrying it home and
having to stand there while her mother
praised it, however awful it was, then stuck it
on the fridge door for the whole world to see.

And after that, Anneli hated having to look at it every morning over her cereal while it got grubbier and grubbier, until the sticky tape at last dried up and mercifully it fell off and slid out of sight under the fridge.

She hated other people's art as well. In the school corridors, she turned her eyes away from the bright splashes of colour pinned on the walls. When children's art was on the television she clutched her belly, pretended to throw up or switched straight off.

Class trips to the local art gallery made her squirm.

'Look at that!' Miss Pears would say to them. 'Isn't that *breath-taking*? Have a good peep at the brush work. Don't we all wish that we could paint like *that*?'

'No.'

'Yuk.'

'Well, she got *paid*.'

Yes, Anneli really hated art. Miss Pears turned back with the freshly mixed pink and Anneli wiped the grumpy look from her face; but a scowl still sat in her heart as she dabbed and poked and scraped about with the bald old paintbrush, trying to use up a bit of the extra pink anywhere there was room so as not to seem rude, but longing for the bell to ring and release her.

Brrrrrrr!

'Heavens!' Miss Pears was astonished. 'The bell! We haven't even begun putting away. Oh, dear me!'

Anneli sighed. It happened every week. Everyone knew the bell was going to ring, and nobody warned her. They all preferred ten minutes of clearing up the art materials to ten extra minutes of whatever might come after. It was a gamble. You might be lucky and miss maths. But, then again, you might miss wonderful, peaceful, almost-as-good-as-being-back-home silent reading.

Today Miss Pears waited till they were all tidy again and then she said:

'And now I want to talk to you about raising a little more money for the new Art Room.'

Anneli groaned. Why did Miss Pears want to go on about that again? Hadn't they given enough of their pocket money, and wheedled enough out of their parents to build a new Art Room out of gold bricks and equip it with diamond-studded easels and ermine paint-rags?

Perhaps there were now plans to fill the paint pots with molten silver?

Anneli came out of her grumbly daydream long enough to hear Miss Pears saying the words 'need even more money'.

Oh, no. Not more! They'd reached the class target three times already. But Miss

Pears was mad on painting, and clearly wouldn't stop.

'I don't want you to go running to your parents, who have enough strains on their purses. Let's think of things to do ourselves. Can anyone think of any ways of making a little money? No one? Henry?'

Anneli slumped on her folded arms and shut her eyes. She heard good old Henry droning on about baking cakes to sell in break-time, and being paid to sweep up dead leaves and looking for precious old forgotten things in attics. Then Henry's drone seemed to turn into the sound of waves lapping a sunlit shore, and she was miles away, knee-deep in salty water, her arms speckled with gritty golden sand, her eyelids spangled with glistening water drops.

Surina brought her back by asking, 'What are you going to do, then?'

'What?'

'To make money. What are you going to do?'

'Nothing.'

'*Nothing?*'

'Oh, I don't know,' said Anneli irritably. 'I'll think of something.'

And think she did, all the way home.

It wasn't so easy. After all, if money were so easy to come by, someone smart would already have scooped it up. It was all very well to talk of selling cakes at break-time. But Anneli's mother came home from work far too worn out to start to bake for other people.

What about Jodie? Jodie and her little boy Josh lived in the top half of the house, and just as Anneli's mother looked after Josh whenever Jodie had to work in the evenings, so Jodie was in charge of Anneli when Anneli's mother was teaching dance classes at the Leisure Centre.

Would Jodie help her bake cakes?

Probably she would. But she'd have to let Josh help – she was his mother, after all – and Josh was only two and a half. He was a messer. He'd drop the egg shells in the cake mixture, and fiddle with the oven dial so the cakes cooked too slowly, or too fast. He'd spoon the runny icing over the tops while the cakes were still too hot, and put the cherry halves on upside down.

He'd ruin the whole batch. Anneli knew it.

She reached the corner.

The great wrought-iron gates guarding the driveway that led up to Carrington Lodge were padlocked shut, as usual. As usual, Anneli stopped, dropped her school bag and clutched the bars, peering inside. The Lodge was now a children's home, and sometimes, in fine weather, the children could be seen in the gardens, some lying on rugs on the lawns, some rushing around in their wheelchairs, some being carried to and fro by paid helpers like Jodie.

Anneli liked to wave, if they were there. They always waved back, if they could. They all knew Anneli because Jodie sometimes took her and Josh along.

Today there was no one in sight. Only the drive and what little could be seen of the long sloping lawns, and the six great holly trees shading the high stone wall behind. No point in hanging about. Anneli picked up her bag and strolled on, into her own street, her thoughts turning back to Henry and his ideas for making money.

Cake baking might be out, but what about the other two ideas? What were they, now? Oh, yes. Sweeping up leaves. Ridiculous! Anneli hadn't seen a dead leaf in months.

And looking for precious things in attics.

What attics?

Anneli sighed. Honestly, sometimes Henry was hopeless. She might as well go home and ask her mother's advice about raising money – yet *again*.

As she came up the path between the two houses, Anneli caught sight of Old Mrs Pears' pale face at one of next-door's upstairs windows.

Old Mrs Pears waved.

Anneli waved back, politely feigning a happy smile. When your own teacher's grandmother lives next door, you don't take chances.

Safe in the porch, her smile dropped away like a discarded mask, and moodily pushing the door open, Anneli walked in.

2

'Got an attic!'

Behind the door, Josh was waiting with his thumb in his mouth and the purple velvet cloth he loved clutched in his fist as usual.

'Hello, Josh.'

''Lo.'

He followed Anneli along the hall and into the kitchen. Here, Josh's mother was busy cooking.

'Hi, Jodie.'

'Hello, Anneli. Good day?'

But Jodie didn't wait for Anneli to answer because the sharp smell of burn had suddenly risen from the pan and started to fill the kitchen. Hastily Jodie turned her back and started furiously stirring.

Anneli was curious. 'Is supper going to be very early?'

'No,' Jodie told her. 'It's just that it's my turn to cook but I have a most important meeting just before.'

'About Carrington Lodge? And the children?'

'Yes.' But, though she looked worried, Jodie didn't go on to explain. In any case, she was busy rattling through the drawer in search of the bread knife. 'Here, Anneli. Do me a giant favour and make a couple of sandwiches to keep you and Josh alive till supper.'

Josh stood in the doorway, holding his precious purple cloth to his cheek as he watched Anneli carefully slice the loaf. As she spread peanut butter, she asked Jodie, 'Will Mum be home soon?'

'Not for another hour. Someone was sick so Helen's had to stay to teach another class.'

'Oh.' Anneli's disappointment was

intense. She slipped off the chair. 'I'll go and read, then.'

Jodie looked up from the sauce that was proving so tricky. 'You couldn't be an angel and take Josh with you? Keep him happy just for a few minutes, till I get all this lot sorted.'

Anneli sighed. But still she let Josh follow her along the hall and into the sitting room. It was impossible to read your own book when Josh was about. He always wanted you to read to him instead. So while she was rooting through the bookshelves, looking for something that they both enjoyed, she asked him amiably, 'So, Josh. What did you do today at playgroup?'

Josh made a face.

'Had to sing songs.'

'You're lucky,' Anneli told him with feeling. 'I had to paint.'

In a surge of sympathy, Josh held

out towards her the velvet cloth, spattered with bread crumbs and smeared with peanut butter.

'It's all right,' Anneli told him. 'It's all over now.'

Josh finished his sandwich, then started picking up the bits he'd dropped and eating those.

'Want to go and help Mummy?' Anneli suggested hopefully.

'Help *you*,' Josh said firmly.

'Go on, then,' Anneli said. 'Help me. Which shall we do first? Sweep up dead leaves, bake cakes to sell, or find an attic full of precious things?'

Josh looked embarrassed.

'Not got no leaves,' he said. 'Can't cook.'

'Not got no attic, either,' Anneli said bitterly.

Henry's trio of bright ideas had all turned out to be right duds.

'Got an attic,' said Josh.

'Don't be silly. We haven't got an attic.'

'Got an attic.'

'You don't know what an attic is.'

'Do.'

'Don't.'

He stuck his tongue out at her.

'Do.'

Anneli was irritated.

'All right,' she challenged him. 'Show me!'

Instantly, Josh made for the door.

Anneli followed. She never thought that Josh had anything at all to show her, but she went with him as he clambered up the stairs, until he reached the door that separated Jodie's top half of the house.

Anneli pushed it open. Josh walked past his own little bedroom, barely larger than a cupboard, and through the room in which Jodie kept her books, her sewing machine, the television and the stereo. He threaded his way between the armchairs, and grasped the handle on the door to his mother's bedroom.

'You'll catch it,' Anneli warned. 'You're not allowed to play in there.'

'Not playing,' Josh insisted. 'Showing.'

He opened the door.

Going into Jodie's room was, Anneli always thought, like stepping in a magical cavern, or going under water suddenly. The glorious silk shawls draped over the window to hide the wall outside made it glow soft and greeny-blue, like living at the bottom of a goldfish bowl. The room smelt of flowers and joss sticks. Plants trailed and climbed all over, even inside the fireplace with its pretty patterned tiles. Little bells hanging by embroidery silks were jingling softly in the breeze from the window. The floor was bright with rugs, and the bedspread a riot of patchwork.

And scattered all over, on everything, were pretty things: rings that dazzled, bangles that caught the light, earrings that sparkled; small painted jewel boxes, tiny enamelled beads, gleaming glass pots, brass dishes overflowing with strange foreign coins. The walls were bespattered with bright postcards, and a floppy straw hat with scarlet ribbons hung from the bed post.

Everywhere you looked was something you longed to try on, or touch, or stroke, or take the lid off and peep inside.

No wonder Josh was forbidden to play here.

'Go on, then,' Anneli teased him. 'Show me the attic.'

To her astonishment, Josh dived under the bed and disappeared behind the hanging folds of patchwork counterpane.

She heard his muffled voice.

'Come *on*.'

Catching her breath, she knelt and followed him.

Under the bed, it was quite dark and very dusty. Anneli sneezed several times. When she recovered, it was to find that Josh had stuck his purple cloth in her face.

'There,' he said. 'Bless you.'

Anneli pushed the cloth away.

'Where's this great attic, then?' she said a little meanly. After all, her hair was catching in the bedsprings overhead, and pulling. She was bent double. It was too dark to see a thing, and Josh's feet were digging in her stomach.

'There,' Josh proclaimed.

'Where? I can't see a thing!'

'There!'

Josh found one of her hands and pulled it over till it touched the wall behind the bed.

Anneli spread her fingers wide.

Strange. Very strange. It didn't feel like wall. It felt like wooden panelling.

Anneli put out her other hand. Using her fingertips, she traced on the wall the outline of a tiny door.

'What's behind there, then?'

'Attic.'

'It's just the water tank, silly.'

'Attic.'

'It *can't* be.'

Maybe it could, though. Anneli wasn't certain. It was a door. Surely no one would go to all the trouble of putting it there unless there was something behind.

It might be just a water tank. But, then again, it might be an attic.

Only one way of finding out. Anneli made up her mind. There was no point in putting if off. All that would happen was that her imagination would have time to run riot about the dark or the cobwebs or all the awful things the door might hide. If she was ever going to open it and look, it must be now.

She scrambled out from under the bed. Seizing Josh by a leg, she pulled. He came out sliding on a rug.

'You go on down. I'll follow you.'

'Tea time?' asked Josh, ever hungry, ever hopeful.

'Maybe,' said Anneli vaguely. 'Tell Jodie I'll be along in a minute.'

Josh stayed cross-legged on the rug for a few moments, practising the message.

'Anneli 'long in a minute.'

Then he got to his feet and pottered off towards the door.

Before he'd even gone, Anneli had dived beneath the bed again. This time she found the little door without any trouble. Her fingers tightened round the knob. She took the deepest breath.

'Here goes,' she told herself. 'Here goes.'

3
'What a great fizzing cheat!'

The knob turned easily. Anneli pulled the door but nothing happened. She pulled again, harder. The door refused to budge. Anneli tried pushing. The little door swung open so easily it gave her a fright.

A curious musty smell swept out. It was a strange odour of ancient dust and spiders. There was nothing slimy about it. Nothing dank and disgusting. That was a relief. Not daring to delay, Anneli poked her head through. Nothing with creepy long legs fell in her hair. Nothing furry and fast scuttled in front of her.

So far, so good.

She peered into the darkness. Needles of light fell through the cracks in two or three slates. In them, dust motes were spinning. It was a moment or two before she could make out that the floor was rough boards, and above was the sloping underside of a roof.

Anneli peered to the side. On her left, huge and squat like a vast sleeping monster, lay the water tank. A pipe led in at one end and out at the other. The lid was crooked. Anneli shuddered, dreading to think what might have slipped in and drowned, and still be lying at the very bottom. She'd never drink from the bath taps again.

She looked the other way. Darkness. It was impossible to see how far it would be possible to crawl. For all that she could tell, the little passage under the roof might come to a dead end only a few feet away, or might go on forever. It was too dark to see.

She shuffled forward on her knees towards a lump of shadow at the end that might be a corner she could crawl round and keep on going till she found an attic full of precious things. But suddenly behind her there was a huge and echoing clang that startled her so much she froze.

Anneli felt sick with terror. She shut her eyes. Then, suddenly, another noise took over. The sound of rushing, filling water.

Of course! The water tank in action!

Anneli kept her eyes shut till she was absolutely sure. In this dark space, the sound seemed enormous. But already the hissing rush was slowing to a trickle, then droplets running after one another fast, and then, at last, just the occasional drip that sounded round and wet and hollow as if in some ancient cavern underground.

Anneli pulled herself together and carried on.

The lump of darkness turned out to be,

not a corner leading to further passages, but a dead end.

So much for all her bravery. So much for Henry's brilliant idea. Something precious to sell in an attic! How stupid!

Bitterly disappointed, Anneli sat down and leaned back.

There was the loudest of clicks, and then a hideous grating noise. Whatever Anneli was leaning against was giving way. She struggled to regain her balance. A little door, no larger than the one she'd crawled through earlier, was swinging open. Anneli tumbled backwards, catching her elbows on the frame of the doorway and landing on threadbare carpet that scraped her knees.

It *hurt*. Tears pricked behind her eyes. Anneli blinked them shut. But when she opened them again, what did she see in front of her but the most hideous face, glaring at her with fierce hatred.

Anneli shut her eyes tightly again, out of sheer terror, and waited for whoever it was to pounce.

But nothing happened. The moments passed. She could not even hear breathing. Just silence, absolute silence. Had she imagined it all in the great shock of tumbling through the hole? Had she seen what she thought?

She flickered her eyelids open the

tiniest amount. Not quite enough for anyone watching to think she was looking at them. Just enough to let the smallest crack of light seep in between her eyelashes and let her peep a second time.

That face! Still there! But something so odd about it . . .

Anneli's eyes widened. Without being able to prevent herself, she cried out loud:

'What a great cheat!'

It was a painting.

Life-size, and stuck right in her face, it had fooled her into thinking it was real. But it was just a painting, propped up and facing where she fell.

'What a great fizzing *cheat*!'

And then, from the other side of the room, there came a voice.

'*What's* a great fizzing cheat?'

The voice scared Anneli even more than the first sight of the painting. The blood ran cold in her veins. She couldn't answer.

She heard the question again.

'*What's* a great fizzing cheat? Who *are* you? Come on out from behind there, so I can see you. What on *earth* is going on?'

4

'Precious to sell and precious to keep.'

Anneli was no chicken. She'd never found that trying to avoid trouble got her out of it, or made it any easier when it came. She'd never believed in ghosts, and she was pretty brave about people, even exasperated ones into whose rooms she fell, uninvited and dusty. So scrambling to her feet, she peered over the large gold frame of the painting.

There, staring back at her was Old Mrs Pears.

'Anneli!' said Mrs Pears. 'How very sweet of you to drop in.'

Anneli grinned sheepishly.

'Are you hurt? Are you horribly bruised? That was a thump and a half.'

Anneli prodded the worst bits.

'Not too bad,' she said. 'I'll be all right.'

'Did you bring Josh along with you? Or is he lost somewhere in the roof?'

'No,' Anneli said. 'It's only me. And I was hoping to find something precious.'

Mrs Pears looked about the room, and gave a vague but gracious wave of invitation.

'Oh, no!' said Anneli hastily. 'I didn't mean from you!'

'Of course,' said Old Mrs Pears, speaking softly, as though to herself and not to Anneli, 'there's precious to sell and precious to keep, and in this room, I'm afraid, there's mostly precious to keep.'

Anneli looked about her. The room itself was the mirror image of the room she'd crawled from, Jodie's bedroom. There was the same bow window, the same cupboard doors, even the same old-fashioned fireplace with its pretty blue patterned tiles.

But this room could not have looked more different. Where Jodie's room was filled with cosy, pretty things, this room was filled with paintings. Paintings hanging on every spare inch of wall, and propped above the mantelpiece, and leaning in stacks against the cupboard doors, and laid flat on the desk. Dozens of paintings in dozens of frames, simple and fancy. Everywhere you looked were drawings and paintings – snarling animals, blossoming trees, fast flowing rivers, beautiful women in long white dresses lifting their parasols against the sunlight, men fighting battles, women weeping, a little girl sitting on a bench nursing a black and white rabbit.

Art. Everywhere you looked. Nothing but art.

'Did you *buy* all of them?' demanded Anneli, far too aghast at the thought of such a massive waste of money to remember her manners.

'Lord, no,' said Mrs Pears. 'My brother painted them.'

'*All* of them?'

'Every last one.'

'What *for*?'

Mrs Pears stared at Anneli, and then asked, very politely:

'Anneli, do you know very much about art?'

'Nothing,' said Anneli,

'You don't draw, or paint, or go to galleries, or look at books of prints?'

'We slosh about a bit on Tuesday afternoons,' Anneli offered helpfully. 'But that's about it.'

'And do you enjoy it?'

'Not much,' said Anneli, then added with a flash of truthfulness: 'Actually, I hate it.'

Mrs Pears waved her hands around in the air, as though seeking the right words.

'So, when you say: "What for?", what you mean is: "Why did your brother waste his time painting when he could have been doing something else?"'

Anneli blushed.

'I suppose so.'

'And not what many others ask, which is: "Why, when he clearly had talent, did your brother spend so much time copying other artists' paintings?"'

'Is that what he was doing?'

Mrs Pears sighed.

'It was.'

Anneli looked around her, and breathed out slowly.

'He certainly copied an awful lot of paintings.'

'He certainly did.' Mrs Pears let herself down into the chair by the fireplace.

'And he certainly copied a lot of awful paintings, too.'

She shut her eyes, as if to blot out the memory of some of the worst.

'But why?' asked Anneli.

'He wanted money.' Mrs Pears sighed. 'My brother wanted as much money as he could lay his hands on.'

'What for?'

'For his Running-Away Box.'

Anneli was shocked. A Running-Away Box? It sounded almost desperate.

'Why? Was your brother *horribly* unhappy?'

There was a silence. Mrs Pears tilted her head back against the chair, her eyes still closed, her hands folded in her lap. Finally she said:

'Be a dear, Anneli. Run away home. Come back tomorrow and I'll find you something precious to sell.'

5

'Not painting again!'

Anneli sat in bed, trying to concentrate on her library book. But she couldn't read. Her eyes skimmed over the words, but inside her head things were distracting her. Old Mrs Pears, all of those paintings, the brother with his Running-Away Box. It was a mystery, and once there was any sort of puzzle in her life, Anneli could never rest until she had solved it.

When her mother came in, Anneli laid down the book.

'Good day, sweet?'

'It was Tuesday,' Anneli reminded her mother, scowling.

'So?'

'So we had art.'

'And what did you paint?'

Anneli thought back. She could still see clearly in her mind's eye Mrs Pears' brother's paintings – the one that scared her out of her wits, the lovely lady with the frills and the lap dog, the terrified horse – but the large sheet of paper that she herself had worked on for most of the afternoon was no more than a misty blank.

'Something stupid. I can't remember.'

'You never can. You're a real art hater, Anneli. I don't know why I keep bothering to ask you!'

Her mother kissed her and left the room, yawning. Anneli lay back and listened through the half-open doorway. She heard her mother filling the teapot and turning over the pages of the paper. Usually the sounds lulled her to sleep, but tonight was different. Though she was tired, her mind was racing, and she was still awake when Jodie let herself in.

'Well?' she heard her mother ask her friend. 'How did the meeting go?'

Anneli heard Jodie sigh. Then:

'Terrible. Terrible. They're going to close the pool.'

Anneli jack-knifed upright in bed. She couldn't believe it! Close the swimming pool at Carrington Lodge? Why, swimming was the only real pleasure some of those children had! They did lots of it, too. It was good for their bodies. On the days Jodie took Anneli and Josh, Anneli saw children who could barely walk, or manage their wheelchairs, moving around in the water as though there was almost nothing the matter with their spines or their muscles or their disobedient legs.

Anneli's mother was just as shocked.

'Close the pool? What? For ever?'

'No, not for ever. Just for a year or so.'

'A year or so! That might as well be for

ever for some of those children!' Anneli's mother said bitterly.

'I told you it was a terrible meeting.'

Anneli heard the sofa springs sagging as Jodie settled.

'It seems that pool's quite ancient. The bottom's giving way, the heating unit is too old for safety, the changing rooms are going mouldy, and the lights need rewiring. They've decided to repair the whole lot all in one go; but none the less it will take months and months.'

'But, Jodie, what about the children? Can they use the pool in town?'

'They can. And they will. But only at certain times of day. And since the minibus can only hold four wheelchairs at one time, there won't be much swimming for anyone this year.'

'Unless they get another minibus.'

'On top of all the repairs to the pool?'

'Have a collection!'

'We only just finished the *last* collection. People round here aren't *made* of money.'

There was a gloomy silence. Anneli rolled over and bunched the duvet up over her head. Cracked pools and mouldy changing rooms. Only one minibus. Art rooms. Everyone needed money for something. She simply didn't want to hear another word. She'd think about it all tomorrow . . . tomorrow . . .

Tomorrow turned out to be the oddest day, and not one on which Anneli found time to think much at all. When she reached school in the morning, she found Henry doubled over the gates, waiting for her, shrieking the news.

'Miss Pears is off.'

'Off?'

'Not coming to school.'

'That's never happened before. Perhaps she's feeling sick.'

'Perhaps she's ill.'

'Perhaps she's *very* ill.'

'Perhaps she's dying.'

'Perhaps she's dead.'

'Perhaps she's buried.'

'Don't be so silly. Who are we getting instead?'

'No one. There isn't anyone, so they're splitting us up. Everyone else is having five of us. We're to be helpers.'

'Teaching babies the ABC?'

'You won't be any use, then. You don't know yours yet.'

The insults kept up through the ringing of the bell, and standing in line. Anneli was smart. Grabbing Henry, she fought her way to the front. The deputy head would split them into fives. If Mrs Fleming had any sense, she'd pick the quiet goody-goodies

queuing at the front, dying to get into school, to join her in the infant class.

And since Anneli liked Mrs Fleming and didn't mind infants, she was determined that she and Henry would get into Mrs Fleming's pack of five.

It paid off. Soon she and Henry were being swept away in a tide of little people.

Mrs Fleming, it was clear, had no idea what to do with the five she had picked. She looked around the room searching for an idea. Anneli watched with horror as her eyes settled on the six easels in the painting corner, the aprons, the jam jars filled with bright poster paints.

'Art,' she said firmly. 'That'll be nice.'

'No, it won't,' Henry said loyally. 'Anneli hates art.'

'*Painting!* Not painting *again*!'

'We had art yesterday.'

'Painting? All *day*?'

'On those silly easels?'

'I'm certainly not wearing one of those bibs!'

Mrs Fleming lifted her hand for silence.

'You five can stay in that corner together and paint quietly,' – she paused – 'or I can send up for a set of long division cards.'

The complaining quietened to a sullen muttering, and then, as Henry handed round the brushes, squabbling broke out instead.

'I can't paint with this. This brush is *bald*. I might as well paint with my *fingers*.'

'I've seen your work. I thought you did.'

'This brush has exactly seven bristles left in it.'

'Let *me* count.'

'Careful!'

'Whoops. Sorry.'

'Now there's only six!'

Anneli dragged her easel backwards until it stood right behind Henry's, and she could see what he was doing. She waited while he stared at his blank sheet of paper, deciding what to paint. Henry never drew anything in pencil first. He said that the lines always spoiled it after. He simply thought for a long while instead.

As she stood watching, Anneli found

herself filling with curiosity. What was he going to paint? Which colour would he begin with? Would his brush strokes be bold and slashing, or dotty and delicate? She waited, burning with impatience, for him to start.

Then, at last, Henry dipped his brush into a jar of light blue. Anneli did the same, moving as far as possible like an action replay on the television. Henry drew his brush firmly across the sheet of paper. With a growing feeling of interest, Anneli did exactly the same.

She'd never taken to art, but this was something different. It was going to be a long morning. So she would do what Mrs Pears' brother had been so good at doing – copying other artists' work.

6

'My garden and my pool.'

At break time, everyone crowded round the two finished paintings.

'Which one is Henry's?'

'This one. It's got his name on it.'

'But that one has, too.'

Anneli grinned. She had enjoyed herself enormously. She'd found it fascinating, and for the first time in her life she'd had a paintbrush in her hand without feeling irritable. From time to time during the morning, Henry had stepped back to admire her work, and now it was finished he did so again.

'That's very good.'

'You did it.'

'But you painted it.'

'But it's your painting.'

Henry screwed up his face.

'Funny, that. Whose is it, then?'

Everyone had an opinion.

'Yours.'

'Hers.'

'Mine.'

'His.'

'Both of ours.'

Henry asked Anneli:

'Was it difficult to do?'

'Not really,' Anneli said, 'once I got into the swing of painting like you do. It was easier when I didn't try to keep up. When you were stabbing away at those tree tops I couldn't stab as hard and as fast as you did in case you weren't making them the shape I thought. So I waited till you'd finished, and then did them all in a rush, like you, after.'

'They came out just the same,' Henry admitted admiringly.

'Almost,' said Anneli, ruthlessly self-critical. 'Not quite.'

Henry leaned over and pointed to her version of the painting.

'See that red there. It's wrong.'

'Your red had white in it. It wasn't like mine. I kept trying to add just the right amount to get it exact.' Anneli ran her finger over the red of her barn roof. 'But it didn't come quite right until I got here.' She pointed again. 'I tried going back and painting over, but that made it look too thick, so I had to stop.'

'You can see where you've gone over it twice.'

'Only because you've been told.'

'Maybe.'

'The worst,' said Anneli, 'was the geese.'

'Yes, geese *are* difficult to paint,' said Henry complacently.

'It wasn't that,' Anneli assured him.

'It's just that I could hardly bring myself to do them. It was such a *mistake*, don't you think, sticking them all over the grass and sky like that, flapping their wings.'

For a moment, Henry just stared. But by the time he'd leaped to his feet and started after her, she was already half way towards the girls' lavatories, and both the paintings had been whipped away by the wind.

Mrs Pears was astonished that Anneli came to the front door.

'Sorry to take such an age,' she said. 'I admit to waiting for you upstairs, by the hole.'

Anneli went scarlet.

Mrs Pears led the way into the sitting room, and sat on the sofa. She patted the space at her side, and Anneli sat down. A tray of tea things lay in front of them on a

low table, and there were chocolate biscuits.

Anneli told her everything. She told how she had lain in bed the night before and heard Jodie coming home from her meeting at Carrington Lodge. She told about the cracks in the bottom of the pool and the failing heating unit, the unsafe wiring and the mouldy changing room. She told Mrs Pears how the children so enjoyed their time in the water, and how the pool was going to be closed for a whole year.

'A whole year?' The old lady's face softened with memory. 'Why, it took only half that time to build in the first place!'

Anneli was astonished.

'How do you know?'

'Because I remember very well. I remember as if it were yesterday.'

'Were you there?'

'There? I watched every day, from dawn till dusk. Behind my back, the workmen called me The Shadow.'

'They let you in the garden?'

'It was my garden.'

'*Your* garden?'

'My garden and my pool. The pool was built for me. It even has my initials built in it. When you were visiting, didn't you ever notice the fancy initials on the side of the pool, down at the deep end?'

'Those tiny blue and green tiles?' Anneli recalled treading water and tracing them with her fingertips, wondering about them. Each letter was the size of her hand, so curvy and elegant and old-fashioned, it was hard to be sure which letter it was. 'There was an A, I remember. I loved the curly legs on the A.'

'C. A. M. C-S. That's what the letters are. My name – or, rather, my old name before my marriage: Clarissa Amelia Mary Carrington-Storrs.'

Anneli stared.

'And now you're Mrs Pears.'

'And the house in which I grew up is a home for children.'

'But it's a *lovely* house!' Anneli burst out. She remembered so clearly and with such pleasure her afternoons in its wild gardens. 'Why did you ever, *ever* leave?'

Mrs Pears sighed and smiled and inspected her fingernails closely.

'Ah,' she said. 'And so we come back once again to the tale of my brother.'

'Tell,' Anneli said. '*Please* tell.'

So Mrs Pears told.

7

'He was forbidden.'

'When I was young,' Mrs Pears told Anneli, 'my father was very rich indeed. He ordered Carrington Lodge to be built. My mother designed the garden. Gardeners did the work, but my mother gave the orders: a summer-house here, a rose-trellis there, an orchard and tall holly trees to hide the stable wall.'

She sighed.

'It's changed a lot. They've taken up the crazy paving and laid down concrete paths for the wheelchairs. And our old gardeners would have a fit if they saw the flower beds now. But the grounds are still lovely and you can still almost get lost in them.'

'Oh, yes,' said Anneli. 'I almost have.'

'There were four of us in the family.

My brother was called Tom, and he was older. He was away at school most of the time.'

'Who did you play with?'

'No one. I played alone. I wasn't lonely, though. I made up friends, imaginary friends, and played with them.'

'Were you happy?' asked Anneli, remembering Tom's Running-Away Box.

'Oh, I was happy; but my parents worried so. They'd watch me offering to share my toys with empty air, or overhear me answering unasked questions, or catch me laughing at nothing, and they became so anxious, so anxious . . .'

'They built the swimming pool, to distract you.'

'How clever you are!'

'Just a guess,' Anneli said modestly.

'I watched from the day the first men came to measure to the day the last coat of glaze was painted over the tiles. I was never allowed to sit on grass in case I took a chill. Colds could be dangerous in those days. So we sat on the bench – all my imaginary friends and myself – and watched our pool take shape in front of us.'

'Didn't Tom ever watch with you?'

'Oh, no. Even during his holidays, Tom was always busy. He'd taken a passion for painting, and spent all day and evening in the conservatory, painting and painting. He'd leap off the school train acting like someone starved for the smell of oil paint and turpentine.'

'Didn't he paint at school?'

Mrs Pears laughed.

'They hadn't much time for art in Tom's sort of school!'

Privately, Anneli thought this no very bad thing. But she said nothing.

'The moment he came home, he

snatched up his brushes and barely laid them down again till he left. He painted anything and everything. He even painted me. Do you remember the painting of a girl in frilly skirts sitting on a bench nursing a black and white rabbit?'

'Yes. I saw that one.'

'Well, that was me. I sat still for hours. The rabbit became quite testy, and nibbled me badly.'

'Did you make Tom pay you?'

'*Pay* me?' Old Mrs Pears raised an eyebrow. 'Heavens! It would never have occurred to me even to *hint* at the idea.'

'Unless they were paid, no one in my class would sit still to be painted.'

'Even by their own brother?'

'*Especially* by their own brother.'

Mrs Pears said, 'How times do change.' She stared down at the biscuits, remembering. 'I think that I was very proud to be asked. Usually he painted other sorts of pictures entirely.'

'Sunsets and rivers and battles and petunias and tigers,' said Anneli, recalling some of the paintings upstairs.

'Rivers were fine,' said Mrs Pears. 'There are three rivers within easy cycling distance of the Lodge.'

'No tigers, though.'

'No battles, either. But there were sunsets and petunias. And that's how the trouble began. Because Father was a little uneasy about Tom's passion for painting. He was a plain man, you understand. He'd mixed with plain men all his life, even though he had made money and he'd married more. And in those days a plain man didn't think it quite right for his one and only son and heir to spend his days painting pink sunsets and petunias. It made Father most uncomfortable. He thought it girlish.'

'Like thinking it was unladylike for girls to be explorers.'

'Exactly. Though Mother, of course, wasn't anxious about that. She was too busy fretting because her daughter sat on a bench the live-long day watching a hole dug deeper and deeper, and whispering to invisible people.'

'You sat and sat?'

'I sat and sat. And in the end Tom said: "If Clarrie's just sitting on a bench all day anyhow, she can make herself useful and sit for me. I'll paint her." So he carried his easel out to the garden and ordered the maid to look out my frilliest dress. He fetched the most biddable rabbit from the hutch, and began to paint. And since I was determined not to stop watching the workmen, he had to set his easel up beside the hole.'

'Wasn't that in the way?'

'Indeed it was.'

'Didn't the workmen mind?'

'Oh, they minded. But then, as now, a workman would put up with anything if he was glad to have the work. Both of us were in the way. Tom was a nuisance with his easel and clutter and fussing about shadows. But I was worse.'

'How? You were only sitting there, after all.'

'But if any one of those poor men stopped and leaned on his spade for a moment, I'd be calling: "Why have you stopped? What's the matter?" It wasn't that I minded their taking a break. It was that I was worried they'd come across some snag – bedrock, quicksand, a swamp – anything that might prevent my pool being finished. I didn't mean to be forever urging them on. Lord, no. But I suppose I had the same effect on them as if I did. And gradually they became less friendly. Then almost sullen. And towards the end, though they were never actually *rude*, they took to getting their own back in quiet little ways.'

'What ways?'

'They'd pretend not to hear when I called out to them. And if they noticed me chattering to my secret friends, they'd mutter: "Soft in the head," and grin and shake their heads, and screw their fingers to their temples. And whenever Tom came over to shake out the frills in my dress they'd smirk a little behind his back, and flex their huge bronzed muscles, and nudge one another knowingly.'

'Making out Tom was a bit of a pansy.'

Mrs Pears stared at Anneli.

'Well, yes,' she said after a moment's pause. 'I suppose you could put it that way.'

'That's certainly the way they'd put it at our school.'

'Is it, indeed?'

Blushing, Anneli prompted Mrs Pears to return to her story. 'So the workmen were teasing you both.'

'Just a little. But enough to cause trouble as soon as Father noticed. He must have been standing in the shadows for quite some time one day, watching quietly as the workmen sniggered because suddenly he strode out into the sunlight, startling everyone, and bellowing with rage.'

'What did he bellow?'

'I've no idea to this day. I was so terrified that not a word went in. All I know is, the workmen crept off with all their tools, scowling horribly. And on the next day there were four different men, and Tom never painted in the garden again.'

'Never?'

'He was *forbidden*.'

'Forbidden?'

'Forbidden entirely. Oh, it was quite unreasonable, everyone agreed, even my mother, though she only dared hint as much in a whisper. But it was final. My father was so angry that, weeks after, if he so much as came across one of Tom's brushes lying about the house, he'd snap it in two directly. And Tom was told that he could never, *ever* paint in front of other people again.'

8

The Running-Away Box

Anneli was so shocked. 'Did Tom stop painting?'

'Stop painting? Tom?' Old Mrs Pears gave a wry smile. 'As soon tell the wind to stop blowing. He simply set up his easel in his bedroom and started to copy a painting on the wall.'

'Ah,' Anneli said. 'Started to copy.'

This was the bit she wanted to hear.

'That's right. Lots of artists do it. It's a way of improving one's own work.'

'I know,' said Anneli. 'I've done it. Mine improved a lot.'

Mrs Pears looked a little surprised.

'Yesterday you told me you didn't take very much interest in art.'

'I take a bit more now. Starting this

morning.'

Mrs Pears took a deep breath, and continued.

'The house had quite a collection of paintings and drawings. Father bought huge ugly paintings cheap at auctions and hung the horrors all over, and Mother bought lovely delicate drawings from Paris to try to distract attention from Father's worst choices. So there was plenty to choose from when Tom wanted something to copy.'

'And he was good at it.'

'Oh, he was very good indeed. He had a gift. He soon became so deft, so skilled, so *good* at copying, that apart from the fact that the ones on the walls were framed, it was difficult to tell which was which.'

'How *do* you tell?'

After the business of copying Henry, the question interested Anneli.

'Tom always said: "The longer you look at the real thing, the richer and finer it seems and the more life you see inside it. The longer you stare at my copies, the more they seem to shrivel inside".'

'But if they're both the same . . .'

'But they're not. The artist is painting in his own way, just what he wants, from his own soul. He can let go.'

'And the copier can't.'

'Exactly.'

'So *that* was the trouble with my tree tops,' muttered Anneli.

Mrs Pears stared.

'I beg your pardon. Did you mention tree tops?'

'Yes,' Anneli said. 'No. Carry on, please. Didn't Tom paint any more for himself?'

'That painting of me on the bench with the rabbit was one of the last two real paintings that Tom ever did.'

'Can I go up and look at it again?'

'I'll come too,' Mrs Pears said. 'Take my arm.'

It took forever to get up the stairs. Like Josh, Mrs Pears had to take steps one at a time, and clutch the banisters to keep her balance. Anneli burned with impatience. She'd never thought she'd be longing to get a second look at a painting. But she could hardly wait to get up in the room and sort through the canvasses till she found it again.

It was in the corner, behind one just the same size of a middle-aged man with a floppy velvet hat and merry eyes. Compared with that, it seemed a dreamy sort of painting. Gently, Anneli slid it out and leaned it against the desk, in the light from the window.

The little girl seated on the bench in the sunlight looked anxious and forlorn. Her face was pale under her bonnet, and her slim white fingers dug in the fat rabbit's fur in a rather desperate way, as if she feared that he, like everybody else, might hop away from her at the first chance. A slight flush on her cheeks hinted to Anneli that the dress must have been a horror to wear – all stiff and stuffy. And there was something else. A little ring of rash circled Clarissa Amelia Mary Carrington-Storrs' narrow neck.

Anneli said:

'The lace round the neck of that dress was all prickly!'

'So it was! How I remember! However did you know?'

Anneli leaned forward and pointed to the tiny rash ring.

'My heavens!' said Mrs Pears. 'You're sharp enough to be an art historian!'

'Is that a job?'

'It certainly is.'

'That might be fun,' said Anneli. 'See what people had for supper four hundred years ago.'

'And if they had rats running round the kitchen.'

'And if they wore any clothes in bed. And what they kept for pets.'

'You can even work out what people thought from a painting. Once, women's bodices were worn very low, so people painted them that way. Then people who lived later were so shocked by the old paintings that they paid artists to paint curly ringlets of hair falling over the bare skin, to cover it up.'

'*You* wouldn't have needed any extra ringlets,' said Anneli. 'Your dress was almost up to your ears. Why do the trees behind look funny like that?'

'Tom never managed to finish the painting.'

'What a waste! Was he angry with your father?'

'Angry? He was so angry he started the Running-Away Box. He said he wouldn't stay in the house a week longer than he had to. He was so desperate to make a start saving, he even bullied me into giving him my two gold sovereigns in return for his cricket bat and his stamp collection.'

'But you didn't play cricket!'

'I didn't collect stamps, either. But he was desperate. And he was my brother.'

Anneli wiped the look of amazement off her face. If being brought up rich enough to have a private swimming pool built for you meant you were also brought up to wear heavy prickly dresses in a heatwave and give your treasures to a brother without even thinking to grumble, then she'd give up the pool and take T-shirts and Josh.

'How much were two gold sovereigns worth?'

'They were valuable even then. Nowadays, they're precious.'

'Precious,' repeated Anneli. 'That's what I'm supposed to be after, something precious.' Her face fell. This need to spend her time thinking of ways to raise money kept nibbling at her good spirits. 'It's a real pity your brother spent it all, running away.'

'Ah, that's just the mystery,' said Mrs Pears. 'It seems he didn't.'

'He didn't?'

'As far as we know, Tom never took any of the money with him when he disappeared.'

Anneli could bear it no longer. She reached out and took Mrs Pears' hand in her own. Tugging gently, she steered the old lady towards the armchair.

'Sit down,' she begged. 'Oh, please sit down. Sit down and tell me how Tom ran away.'

9

'Nonsense!'

By summer, the pool was finished. It wasn't all closed in with walls and a roof, as it is now. It was open to the air, and fringed with bushes and climbing plants that the gardeners put in to hide the mud the workmen's boots had stirred up. Tables were laden with wonderful dishes. The champagne flowed. And everybody we knew from miles around was there to celebrate and admire.

Father strode round the gardens, his bushy red beard and whiskers waggling, hearty and welcoming. Mother stood, pink with pleasure, greeting friends and relations. Everyone said how fine the pool and gardens looked. Ladies strolled about under their parasols. Small children raced around the shrubbery bushes, ignoring their nannies.

And Tom stood at his window upstairs, in shadow, watching. He was in no mood to come down and join the celebration.

'Clarissa,' Mother whispered to me. 'Run up and tell your brother to join us at once. These are our guests, and he must play his part in welcoming them!'

But someone else had spotted Tom standing by the window. She was a cousin of Mother's on a rare visit, wearing a hat drooping feathers as wide as fans. She lifted her long skirts a little at the front, and stepped in through the french windows. She made her way up the staircase and along the landing till she found the room where Tom was standing in front of his easel, gazing out at the gardens, all bright with midsummer blooms.

'Tom! How tall you've grown! You're taller than I am!'

Startled, Tom swung round, knocking the table beside him. On it, an ink drawing lay drying. It was Tom's copy of Mother's most recent purchase.

As the table tipped, the drawing slid off. It floated slowly through the air, and Aunt Germaine reached out and caught it.

She turned it the right way up, and looked at it. Then she inspected it with more care. Then she looked up.

'Why, Tom! This is a Larrien!'

Tom grinned with pride.

'It's mine.'

'Yours, Tom? You mean you *own* it? It's not your father's?'

Tom laughed.

'It certainly isn't my father's. It's mine.'

'Good heavens!' she said, staring. 'A Larrien all of your own!'

Tom said: 'How do you know that it's a Larrien?' He meant: 'How can you be so sure it's not just a copy of a Larrien?'; but Aunt Germaine would have none of that.

'How do I *know*? I know something about Joseph Larrien, I can tell you. I've visited his studio in Paris. I've seen all his exhibitions in London. I know enough to know it's definitely by Larrien and it's quite exquisite. I love it. I want it. Indeed, I *must* have it, and I'll give you this much for it right here and now, Tom!'

And she emptied her little bead purse upside down on the table.

'Can it be worth more than all that?' she demanded.

Tom stared.

'No,' he said, very slowly. 'It's not worth more than all that. That's for sure.'

'Then it is *mine* now.'

Tom tried. He did try. His voice was

dry and choked, and the money lying on the table was twenty times what he had in his Running-Away Box after weeks of hard saving. But still he managed to say:

'It's not a Larrien. It's just a copy.'

Aunt Germaine swept the pile of money closer towards Tom with the flat of her hand, and snatched up the drawing.

'Nonsense!' she cried. 'It's quite as good a Larrien as ever I've seen. You're only trying to back out of a deal. But it's mine now, and thank you, my darling!'

And, kissing him warmly on both cheeks, she swept out.

'By the way,' she called back. 'Little sister Clarrie is lurking behind this door. She daren't come in and tell you what she's been sent all the way up here to say – that your mother wants you out in the garden, all party manners, at once.'

And she was gone.

Tom spread out his hands. They were dead white, and trembling. He stared at them. Then he lifted his head, and he whispered in horror:

'Clarrie, I think I've just become an art forger.'

10
'A life of crime!'

'A life of crime,' breathed Anneli. 'Started by accident!'

Mrs Pears said:

'It was quite terrible. It went from bad to worse. I was sworn to secrecy, but I suffered terribly from the guilt. Things were so different then, you know. Now, getting away with something like that is seen as rather clever, and people don't sympathise with anyone who spends a fortune on a painting and doesn't even know exactly who painted it. They laugh at them instead. But it was different in those days. All cheating was seen as terrible. Dishonourable. A total disgrace. And he was my brother. I lay awake at nights and sobbed and sobbed.'

'Did no one notice?'

'Notice? My dear, the Great War had begun. No one had time to notice a little girl sobbing herself to sleep, or a young lad painting as if there were no tomorrow.'

'You couldn't make him stop?'

'It was as if the devil had got into him. You've no idea. He worked night and day, copying drawings and paintings. He practically went into business, persuading an uncle on leave from his regiment to pick up a block of very old French paper. He told him French paper was better, and old paper had dried out better; and Uncle had far too much on his mind, fighting a war, to guess Tom wanted it because it was the sort of paper Larrien would have used. And while the war dragged on and on, Tom sat in the old schoolroom churning out Larriens as if they were . . .'

'Lavatory paper?'

'Well, not quite that, perhaps. But one after another. He forged a letter from Father to his school, saying he'd be two days late back at school, and slid away to London. Nobody noticed. Everyone was far too worried about the bad news from the war to pay attention. There, Tom found someone who believed his story about his family selling their pictures to pay off their debts. And from then on, Tom sent a steady stream of forgeries to London.'

'And all the money went into his Running-Away Box.'

'All of it.'

'It must have been a huge box.'

'Not so big. Gold sovereigns are surprisingly small, you know. Not much larger than a ten pence piece.'

'You could get plenty of those in a box.'

'The box was rosewood, lined with purple velvet. It had a silver clasp, and set in the lid was a little silver shield, engraved with T.W. H. C-S.'

Anneli looked blank.

'Thomas William Hubert Carrington-Storrs.'

'*Hubert?*'

'Yes, Hubert. Why?'

'No reason.' Anneli straightened her face. 'Go on.'

'So the months passed. News of the war got worse and worse and more and more men joined the army, even my father and uncles.'

Mrs Pears picked at the folds of her skirt.

'And then Aunt Germaine came to stay.'

'Trouble?'

'Trouble indeed. It wasn't *all* her fault, mind you. For Tom was getting a little full of himself. Everyone said so. They'd no idea why but they could see it.'

'*You* knew, though.'

'Yes. I knew. It was the secret life, swelling his head. He loved the risk. It was a glamorous thing to do, you see, to produce work that was as good as a grown man's, or seemed to be. Why, he'd even seen one of his own forgeries hanging in an art gallery for all to see! Imagine! Tom whispered to me that he felt quite shocked! And Father was no longer around to keep him firmly in place. So when Aunt Germaine arrived and talked about those brave, *brave* men at war –'

'Oh, no!'

'Oh, yes. My brother took it into his head to go for a soldier.'

'But he was *far* too young! Surely they wouldn't let him!'

'But Tom was tall for his age and the need for soldiers was desperate. Nobody looked too closely or asked too many questions.'

'Aunt Germaine must have felt terrible!'

'Perhaps she did. Perhaps she didn't. I've no idea. Neither of my parents ever spoke a word to her again.'

The meaning of this took a moment or two to sink in. Old Mrs Pears sat quietly, picking at folds in her dress with her fingers. At last, Anneli broke the silence.

'How long?'

'Eight months,' said Mrs Pears. 'We waited eight grey, endless, anxious months before the news came of Tom's death in battle. Father was grieved, but proud. Mother was bereft. She wrote to Father that she couldn't bear to pace the same rooms, weep in the same garden where she'd watched her dear Tom growing and playing. As soon as the war ended and Father came home, we sold up everything.'

'They kept the paintings, though.

They never guessed.'

'That Tom had become a forger? No, they never guessed. The paintings were locked up, out of sight, never looked at, and I never said a single word.'

'And then . . .?'

'And then, one day, months after, when the worst of the tears had dried and we could sometimes smile again, the last painting arrived.'

'Tom's last real painting?'

'Tom's last real painting. Entrusted to a fellow soldier who had been wounded so badly it took him months to recover enough to seek us out, and give it to me.'

'To you?'

'It was for me. The note with it said so. It said: "*For Clarrie. All I own. With all my love, your Tom*".'

'What was it like?'

'See for yourself.'

Mrs Pears pointed up above the fireplace.

From the moment she saw the painting, Anneli knew there was something mysterious about it.

But what could be odd about a boring old painting of the view of Carrington Lodge from the gates, the same view

Anneli saw every single school day: the top of the long sloping lawn and the seven great holly trees shading the high stone wall behind.

Now what on earth could possibly be mysterious about that?

11

'Only six holly trees!'

The next morning, Anneli left early for school. Something about the painting above the fireplace was bothering her. There was something *wrong* about it, Anneli was sure.

What it was, she had no idea; but it was bothering her terribly.

Usually, she was so late she had to dash straight past the gates to Carrington Lodge without time for so much as a glance between the iron bars. Today, she stopped and peered through, taking her time, wondering. The garden looked more vivid somehow, in the sharp morning light. The lawns gleamed with freshness. The row of holly trees stood tall, like sentries guarding the wall behind from attack. It was the same as ever, but something was wrong.

Whatever it was, it haunted Anneli all day. The sheets of paper she was writing on kept blurring, and suddenly she'd see, as clearly as if it were there in front of her, Tom's last real painting, then, almost at once, blur back to what she'd seen as she peered between the bars that morning.

What was wrong? What was wrong? The holly trees were taller, of course. But that's to be expected. Trees grow.

Trees grow, to be sure. But only in height. Not in number!

Six hollies. Seven. Which? Oh, *which*?

Six holly trees in the garden. And seven in the painting. *Surely* the painting hanging over the fireplace had seven. *Surely* only six grew in the garden.

No painter worth his salt made that sort of mistake. Certainly not Tom, with his great eye for detail and his skill at copying.

So either Anneli herself must have made a mistake in the counting, or there was a mystery to be solved.

And Anneli didn't believe that she was mistaken. After all, hadn't Mrs Pears called her 'sharp enough to be an art historian!'

As soon as the bell rang for the end of school, Anneli grabbed Henry's arm and dragged him along with her, under the shadow of the walls of Carrington Lodge. They reached the gates and stood side by side, staring inside.

'So?' Henry demanded. 'So?'

'Don't you *see*?' Anneli cried. 'Only six holly trees!'

'So?'

'So Tom put *seven* in his painting.'

'So?'

'So!'

'Maybe he had forgotten how many there were.'

Anneli's lip curled scornfully.

'Don't be so silly. He grew up here.'

Henry's brow puckered. Anneli was right. No one could grow up in a garden and not know its trees.

'We'll have to get in and look, then.'

The gates were easy to climb. It was one curly foothold after another, all the way up and all the way down on the other side.

Anneli and Henry vanished into the shadow of the shrubbery. Carefully they picked their way through. Wet leaves slapped at their ankles. Gradually the thick green gloom was flecked with silver. Shafts of sunlight spilled between the last lilacs, and they reached the edge of the old cobbled stable yard.

Here they stopped.

'Well,' Henry said. 'What do you think?'

Anneli stood and stared at the line of

holly trees, thinking in silence.

It was an art historian's job to work things out from little clues. What possible reason could Tom have had for painting in an extra tree? Was he trying to hide something?

But what?

He sent a message with the painting. *For Clarrie. All I Own. With all my love, your Tom*. What could be clearer than that? It *must* be his sovereigns.

But all there was in front of her was solid wall and great tall holly trees.

Wait a minute! This painting was now so old. How much did hollies grow each year? And which tree was the extra one? And who says walls are always solid?

Suddenly Anneli stepped forward into the sunlight. Henry reached out to pull her back, but she shook him off. She was filled with excitement. Making a huge effort to concentrate, she called

Tom's painting to mind.

It formed obediently inside her head.

'There!' she said, pointing. 'We should be looking at that part of the wall. That's where he painted in the extra tree.'

Henry stepped forward.

'All right, then. Let's find a ladder.'

He led the way to the stables. In the dim light the two of them could see the old horse stalls overflowing with clutter: broken old wheelchairs, half a bicycle, rusty bedsprings and an ancient washing machine, a wheelbarrow, boxes and flower-pots and – right at the very end – a long wooden ladder.

Together, they dragged it out into the stable yard.

Henry laid his end on the cobbles. Anneli raised hers. Henry came over to add his strength. Together they heaved the ladder up against the wall.

'Further along,' Anneli told him. 'It

should be further along, between these two trees.'

Henry scraped the ladder along the wall.

'There!' Anneli cried. 'Stop there *exactly*.'

Henry laid his foot on the first rung of the ladder.

'No you don't,' Anneli told him. 'This is *my* something precious.'

She rushed up the ladder before he could argue. The holly trees on either side had grown so high and spread so wide that she was climbing up into a mass of leaves. It was dark. The fiendish prickles dug through her clothing and caught her hair. She spread her fingers out to feel the wall, and was reminded suddenly of when she first spread her fingers in just the same way to feel the little wooden door in the wall that led to Mrs Pears and all of this.

The stone wall was rough and chilled, and slightly slimy.

'Anything?' called Henry.

'Not yet,' she shouted down. How tall had Tom painted the tree? That was a clue. A little bit taller, she was sure. She'd have to go higher.

'I'm going up.'

'I'm holding on.'

Anneli went higher. She reached up as far as she could. The fingers of one hand suddenly slid over a little ledge.

'I'm going one rung higher.'

'Anything?'

Anneli's whole hand disappeared.

'It's a hole. There's a hole in the wall. But it's half blocked up. There's something in it.'

She reached in. Her fingers fell on something square and hard, wrapped up in oilcloth.

'It's a *box*.'

Her heart turned over from excitement. She pulled. The little wrapped box slid easily towards her, stirring a dank smell of leaf-mould. She tugged it closer. Then, feeling her way back on to the lower rung where she felt safer, she drew the box out of the hole in the wall where it had rested undisturbed for so many years, and hugged it to her chest.

'I'm coming down now.'

She backed down through the mass of prickly leaves, clutching the box tightly, until she reached the ground. Henry was jumping from one foot to another. He took the box from her, unwrapped the oilcloth and held it so that the clasp was facing Anneli.

The clasp was stiff, and took a moment or two to lift. Henry stood by in silence. Then Anneli raised the lid. Inside there lay a thick purple velvet cloth, hiding whatever was beneath. Anneli began to unfold it.

'Josh would love that,' Henry observed. 'He needs a new cloth. That one he's got is practically *threadbare*.'

'She'll give it to him,' Anneli said. 'I'm sure she will.'

The purple cloth lay folded back, revealing a pool of old sovereigns, inches deep. Anneli dipped in her finger and stirred. The coins shifted out of their long sleep uneasily, clinking with resentment.

Anneli picked one out and bit it, hard.

'He was a forger,' she explained. 'Just our luck if he was a counterfeiter, too.'

'Solid?'

'Quite solid.'

'Unlike the wall.' Henry looked up into the leafy mass of holly, a little puzzled. 'It must have taken years and years for these trees to grow wide and high enough to hide that hole in the wall. I can't understand why no one worked it out before. His sister had more clues than you, and it was her garden.'

'She wasn't thinking,' Anneli said. 'She had just lost her brother and she was – bereft.'

They looked at one another over the box without speaking. Then Anneli gently closed the lid.

'It's not ours,' she reminded Henry.

'Pity,' said Henry. 'You deserve it. You were the one to notice the puzzle in the painting, and you were the one to solve it. I've never known you take such an interest in art, Anneli. In fact, I've always thought of you as an art hater.'

'I am an art hater,' said Anneli. 'I'm just more choosy than I used to be about the bits of art I hate.'

12

Private and pleasant, and long ago

Anneli carried the Running-Away Box up the garden path to Mrs Pears' front door. She rang the bell. Mrs Pears seemed to take an age to answer; and by the time she did, Anneli's plans to tell the news gently had dissolved entirely in her excitement.

'See!' she said, laying the box down on the hall table. 'See what I found! Surprise, surprise!'

Mrs Pears gasped, and Anneli knew from the look on her face that even after so many years she'd recognised the little rosewood box at once.

Surprise indeed! Mrs Pears ran her fingertips over the tarnished silver shield with T. W. H. C-S. engraved upon it. A small tear glistened at the corner of her eye. Even before she lifted the lid, she was crying gently.

Anneli leaned over and tipped the sovereigns out on to the table.

'See?' she said. 'Hidden at the bottom. A letter from Tom. To you.'

It was faded and stained. But written quite clearly on the front in that old-

fashioned curly handwriting was: *For Clarrie*.

'He certainly cared about you,' said Anneli. 'I'm not sure that either Henry or Josh would ever bother to write a letter to me. But then again, I wouldn't sit still for them in a prickly dress to be painted, like you did.'

She slipped away upstairs, before the tears could fall faster, to fetch down Tom's last proper painting. She wanted to explain to Mrs Pears how she had noticed there was a mystery, and how she had worked out the puzzle.

She pushed open the door to the room full of paintings. Though it was filled with evening light, from the moment she stepped in she had the sense that she was being watched and, nervously, she left the door open.

Anneli looked round at all the paintings. Horses still cantered down leafy lanes.

Water droplets still spun in sunlight over waterfalls. Ladies still strolled arm in arm between roses.

Anneli gave herself a sensible shake. No one was here. No one was watching.

Carrying a little wooden chair to the fireplace, she climbed up to reach Tom's last painting. Gently she lowered it to the floor, then jumped from the chair. Again the sense of being watched swept over her and, quickly, she spun around.

There, still leaning against the legs of the desk on the other side of the room, was the painting of Clarrie sitting on the garden bench in the white dress, clutching the rabbit.

Anneli stared. It was so strange to think that Clarrie and Old Mrs Pears were one and the same person.

The pale, grave little face stared back.

Anneli suddenly said aloud:

'That's how he saw you, isn't it? And that's how he must have remembered you later, when he was scared and miles from home.'

She came a little closer. It was a fine painting. Every pearl button on the frilly dress was gleaming. Clarrie's hair glinted in the sunlight. The rabbit's fur shone.

'If I had any money,' Anneli told Clarrie, 'and if you were not too precious to be sold, I'd buy you for myself since I'm not really much of an art hater any longer.'

She picked up Tom's last painting and turned to leave. Just as she did so, Mrs Pears appeared in the doorway. All signs of tears had disappeared. Her old face was glowing. Smiling, she stepped in and swung the door back on its hinges behind her.

And there, suspended from a clothes hanger and hanging in dreamy white billows and flounces and gathers and ruffles, was Clarrie's best dress, the dress in the painting, the dress from that summer long, long ago.

'I wanted you to have it,' said Mrs Pears. 'I know it's prickly round the neck and you won't ever want to wear it. But still I wanted you to have it.'

Anneli reached out and took a little of the material between her fingers.

'It's beautiful,' she said. 'Quite beautiful. It's something precious.'

And she did wear it. She wore it all one sunny summer afternoon, sitting on the bench in the garden of Carrington Lodge. The dress was hot and heavy, and prickly round the neck, but Anneli sat still and upright, running her fingers down the fur of Henry's black and white rabbit, keeping him happy in her lap. Around her, children were busy painting. Some stood, some sat on chairs, some were strapped into wheelchairs; but all were working hard, frowning with concentration, sucking the ends of their brushes as they thought, or squinting around the edges of their easels.

It had, of course, been Henry's idea: a painting competition at Carrington Lodge's Summer Fair. Tom's painting would be propped up beside the bench to encourage everyone who entered. Mrs Pears would judge the winner. And at the end of the afternoon there would be a Grand Auction of all the paintings in aid of the new school art room.

'Who'd buy them?' Anneli had asked.

'Mothers,' said Henry. 'Mothers and fathers and grannies. You wait and see.'

As usual, Henry was right. Straight after the judging, Jodie climbed on the wooden ramp that came with the brand new minibus Mrs Pears had bought with

money from Tom's sovereigns. She held up the first of the paintings – the one done by Josh. Anneli stared. In it, she thought, she looked like a dirty white maggot with stick legs. The grass was grey and covered with thumbprints. The rabbit was a large splodge in the sky.

'What am I offered,' Jodie asked the crowd, 'for this very fine painting?'

Henry opened the bidding by offering ten pence. Anneli's mother bid thirty. Henry and Anneli's mother bid against one another till Henry dropped out at three pounds fifty after catching a rather stern look from Miss Pears. Anneli's mother bid ten pence more, and just as she began to smile triumphantly, Jodie broke the only rule of auctioneering that Anneli knew by bidding ten pence more than that herself, and promptly bringing down the hammer.

'Three pounds seventy for that,' said a

very complacent Henry. 'Not bad.'

Josh stood by shyly and proudly, pressing his new velvet cloth to his cheek.

Anneli said suspiciously to Henry:

'I never knew you even had three pounds fifty.'

'I don't,' said Henry. 'I am penniless.'

'But you just bid that much for Josh's painting. It might have been knocked down to you.'

Henry stared.

'Knocked down to me? What? With his mother standing there?' He snorted loudly. 'I was just doing my bit to raise the proceeds a little.'

'What a great fizzing *cheat*!'

Henry grinned.

'There's a lot more to this art business than you think,' he said Anneli.

And he lifted his hand to enter the bidding for the next painting.

Anneli looked at it. It was even worse than Josh's. Her eyes looked like giant nostrils. The dress was one large shapeless blob. The rabbit was falling off the edge of the paper.

Just at that moment Mrs Pears came up, resting on her daughter's arm. Though they spoke softly, Anneli couldn't help but overhear her teacher saying:

'Oh, that is truly *awful*.'

Old Mrs Pears was smiling. 'It is terrible,' she agreed. 'So it's a pity your grandfather isn't still alive. He would have bid a lot for that painting.'

But even as it was, with a bit of help from Henry bidding up the price, the painting went for over four pounds.

Anneli was still standing shocked at Henry's cunning when the photographer from the local newspaper came over to take her picture. Obediently she seated herself once again on the bench, the rabbit in her lap, Tom's painting propped beside her.

Henry ran forward to shake out the frills in her dress. A smile crossed Mrs Pears' face, as though she were remembering something private and pleasant, and long ago.

The photographer focused her lens. Here was a lovely photograph, she thought, but the dress looked a nightmare to wear in such hot weather.

'You must be quite an art lover,' she said to Anneli, and was astonished when they all burst into laughter.

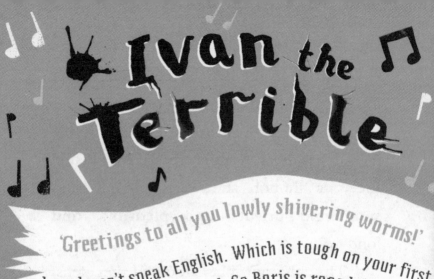

Ivan the Terrible

'Greetings to all you lowly shivering worms!'

Ivan doesn't speak English. Which is tough on your first day at a new school. So Boris is roped in to translate for him. But then the new boy starts threatening to make slaves out of all his schoolmates.

Can Boris keep the teachers happy and Ivan quiet? It's going to be an Ivan the Terribly interesting day . . .

Bill's New Frock

One morning, Bill
wakes up to find
he's a girl. And,
worse, his mum
makes him wear
a pink frock
to school.

Can the day get any worse?
Bill's about to discover
that everything is rather
different for girls ...

'Stylishly written and
thought-provoking'
Guardian

'A gem.'
TES

BILL'S NEW FROCK

ANNE FINE

Illustrated by Mark Beech

THE ANGEL OF NITSHILL ROAD

ANNE FINE

'Anne Fine knows how to make readers laugh' Guardian

'Anne Fine is an author who knows how to make readers laugh'
Guardian

IVAN THE TERRIBLE

ANNE FINE

'Anne Fine knows how to make readers laugh' Guardian

HOW TO WRITE REALLY BADLY

ANNE FINE

'Anne Fine knows how to make readers laugh' Guardian

THE CHICKEN GAVE IT TO ME

ANNE FINE

'Anne Fine knows how to make readers laugh' Guardian

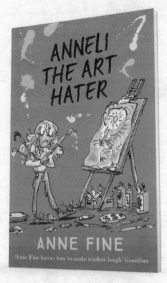

ANNELI THE ART HATER

ANNE FINE

'Anne Fine knows how to make readers laugh' Guardian

Read all of Anne Fine's hilarious stories of classroom chaos

SAVING MISS MIRABELLE

ANNE FINE

'Anne Fine knows how to make readers laugh' Guardian

'Infectiously funny and highly readable' Independent

ON PLANET FRUITCAKE

ANNE FINE